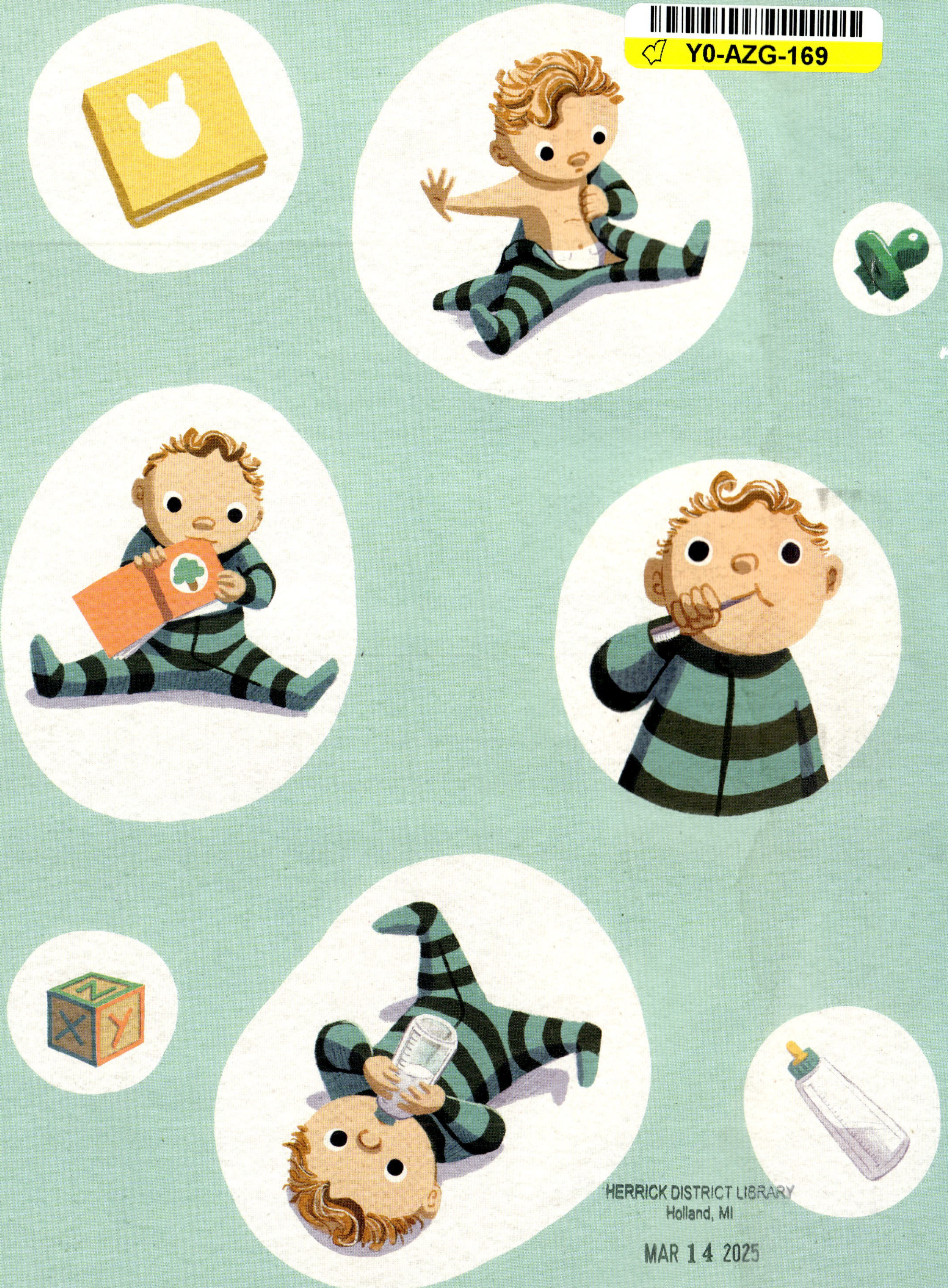

In the light of the moon,
a little baby lay fast asleep.

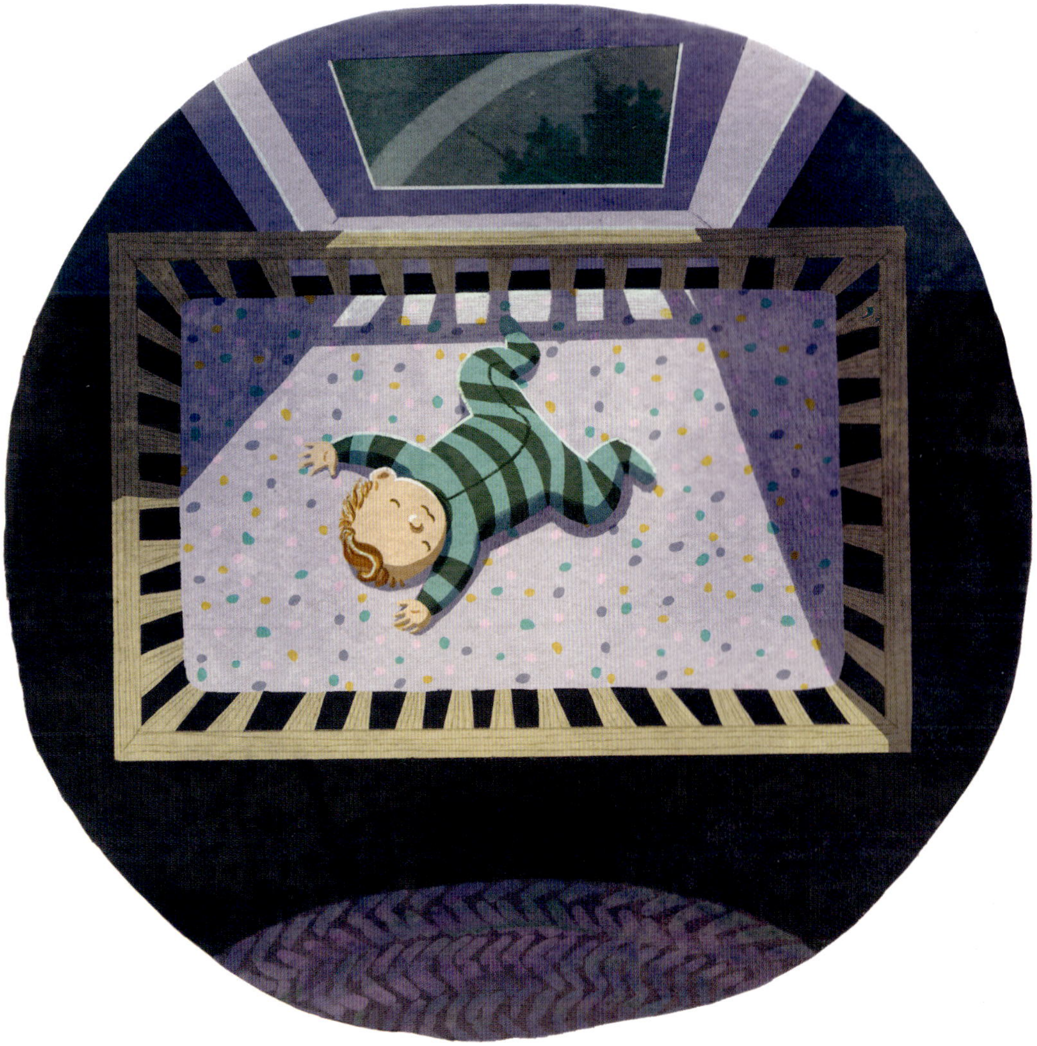

At 8 o'clock, Mama said, "Good night, sweetie."
Papa said, "Sweet dreams, little one."
Sister said, "See you in the morning."

Baby said:

GA!
GA!
GA!
GA!
GA!

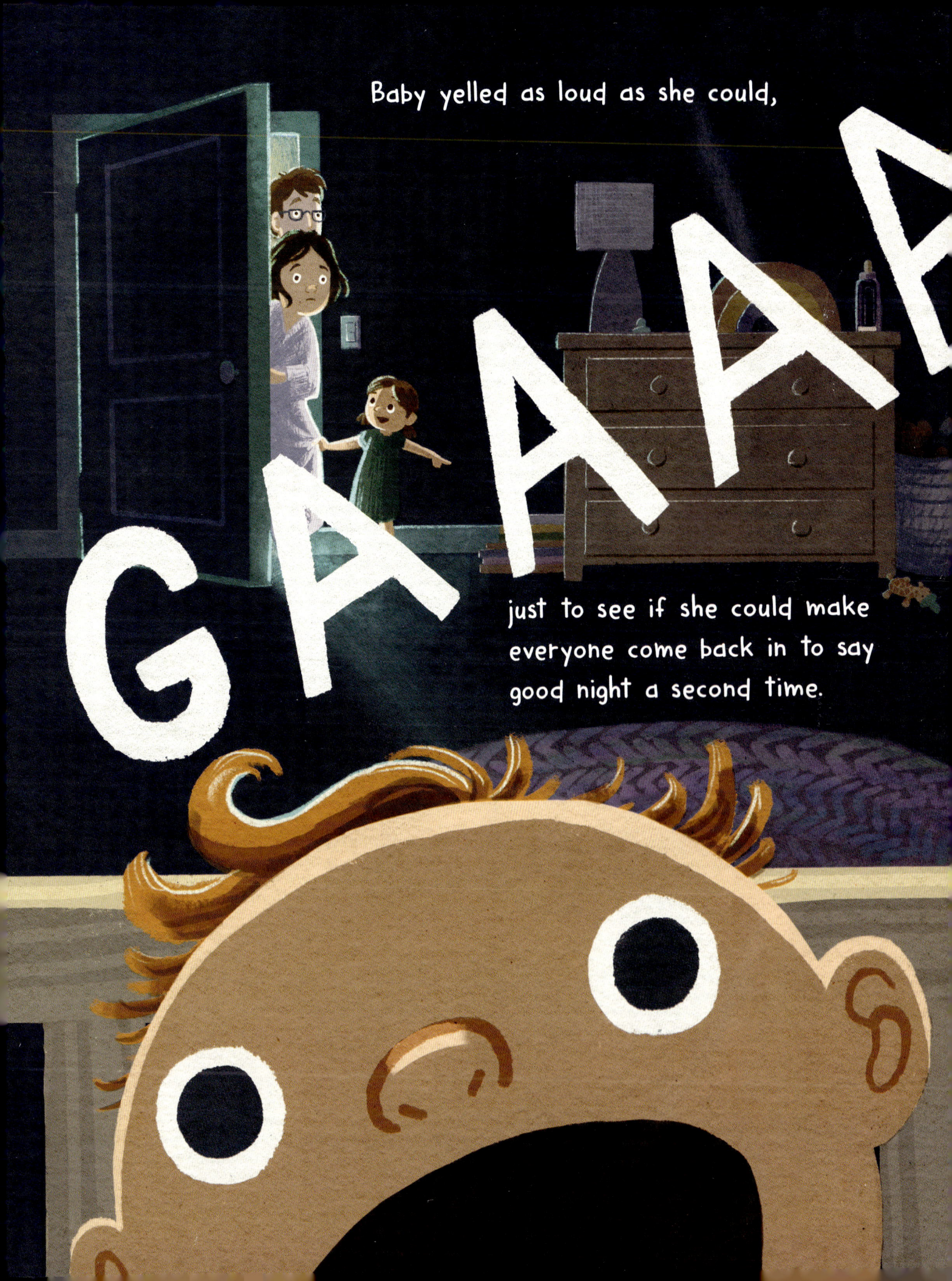

Baby yelled as loud as she could,

just to see if she could make everyone come back in to say good night a second time.

GAAAA

At 9 o'clock,
Mama gave Baby a binky.

Sister gave Baby a binky too.

BAP BAP BAP BAP BAP BAP

And another.
And another.
And another.

HEE HEE HEE

Not even seventeen binkies were enough to make this baby go to sleep.

At 10 o'clock,
Papa cuddled Baby.

Baby explored the inside of Papa's nose.

And Papa's eyelids.

And Papa's mouth.

She found a dangly thing at the back of Papa's throat, but he went back to bed before she could grab it.

At 11 o'clock,
Mr. Neighbor yelled:

IS THAT BABY GOING TO STAY AWAKE FOREVER?

GAAA GAAAAA
GAAAA

Baby was thrilled someone finally understood her plans, so she continued singing the song of her people just for him.

At midnight, no one came to check on Baby, so she decided to do some climbing. She was an excellent climber, because she practiced every night. Baby could climb up things. Baby could climb over things. Baby could—

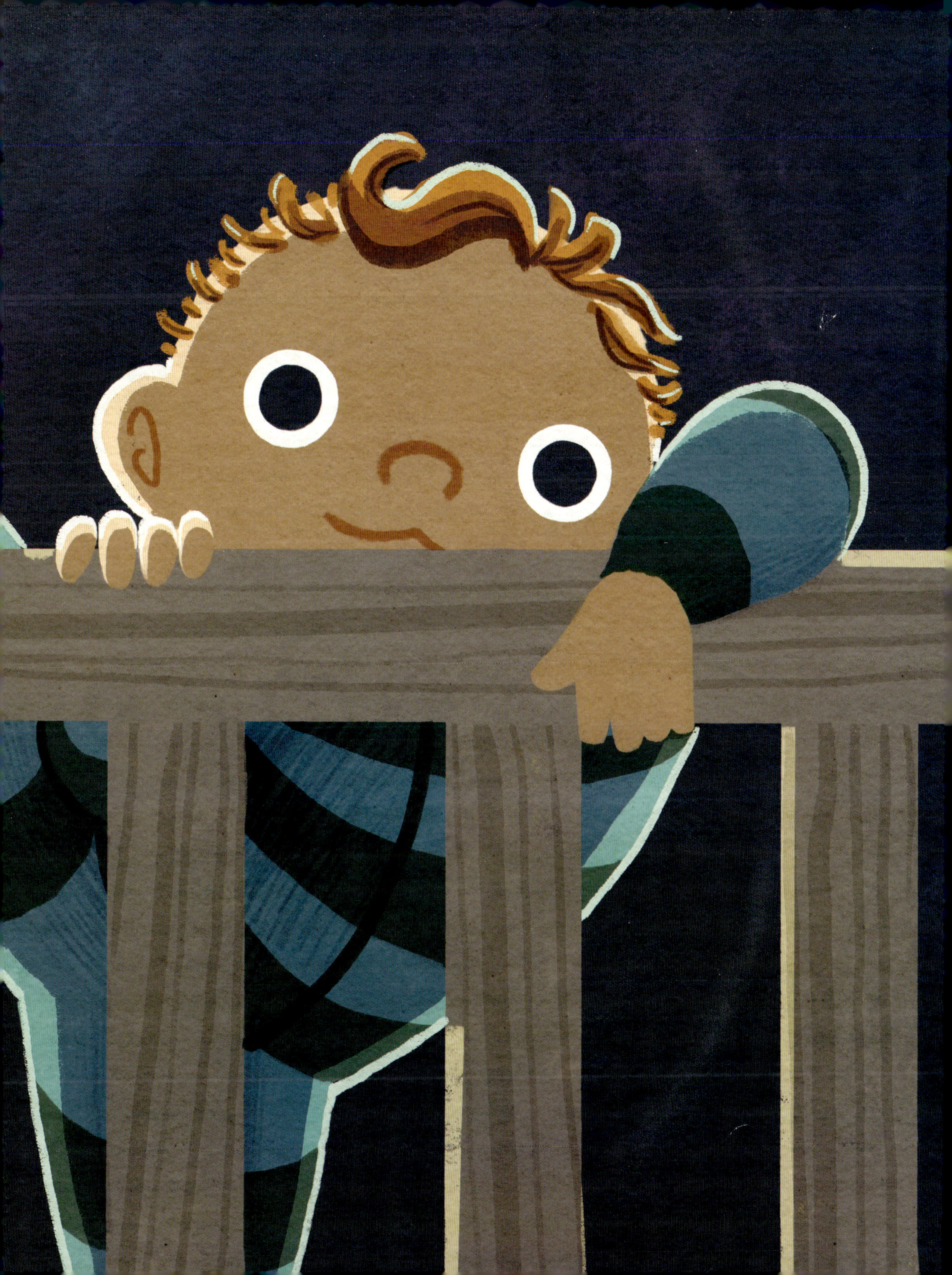

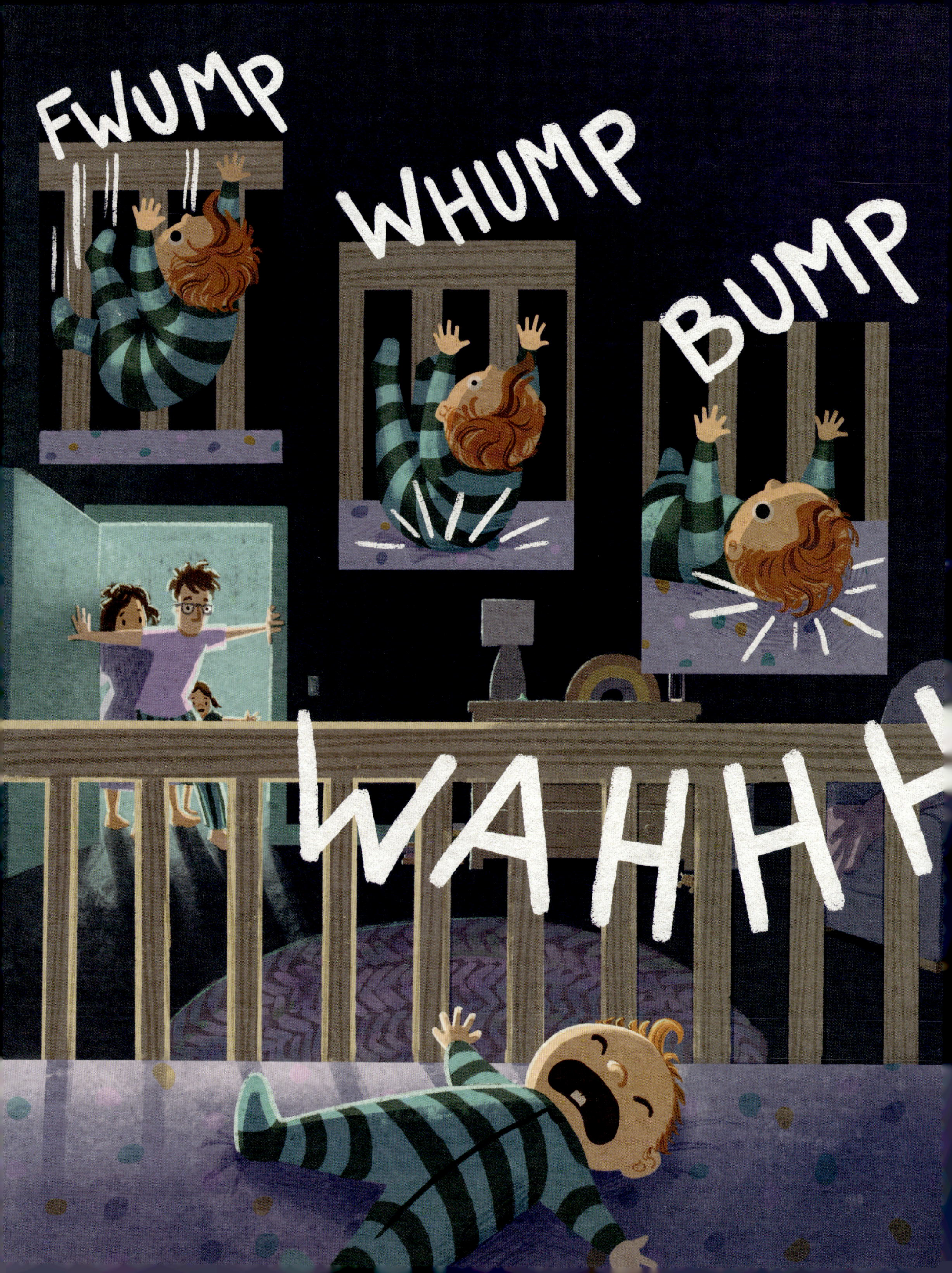
FWUMP
WHUMP
BUMP
WAHHH

Mama cried, "What happened?"

Papa cried, "My poor baby!"

Sister cried, "Oh no!"

Baby just cried. Very loudly. She did not enjoy falling. However, she did enjoy a captive audience, so she kept crying for a very long time . . .

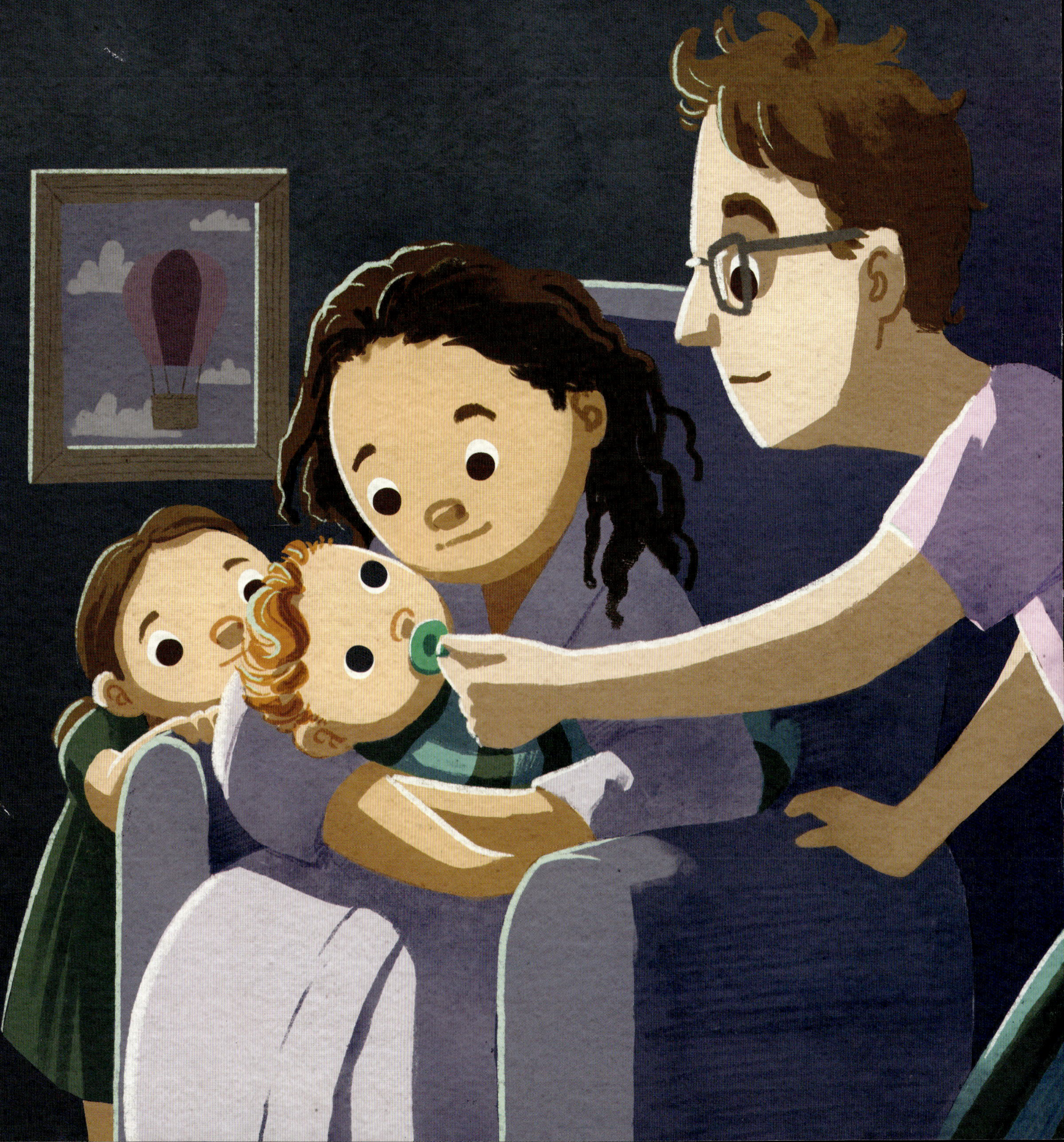

. . . until Papa gave her a binky and Mama gave her a cuddle and Sister gave her a kiss and Mr. Neighbor gave up on sleeping entirely.

Which was probably for the best, because at 1 o'clock, Baby threw a dance party.

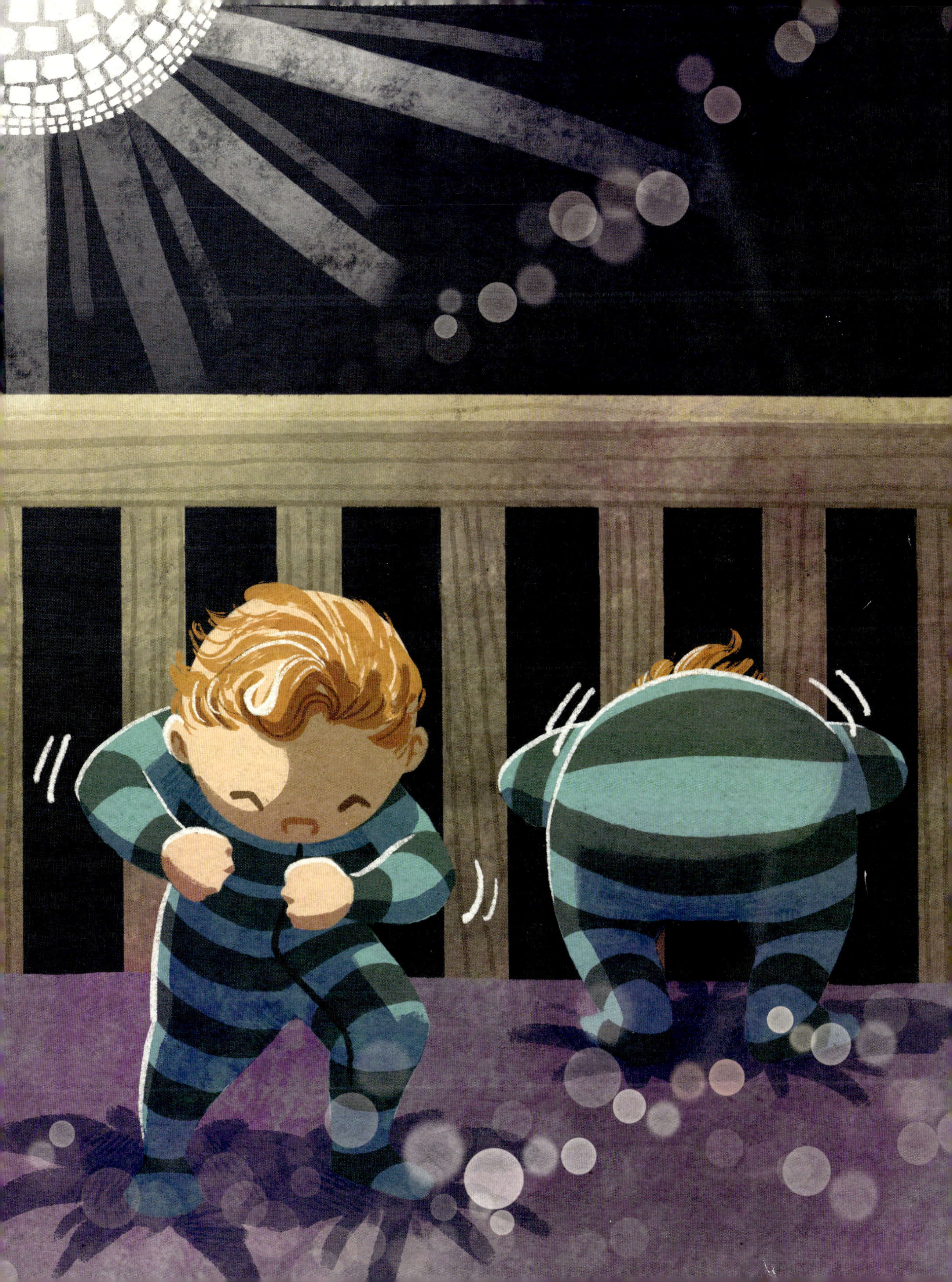

Then, at 1:15, Baby jumped fifty times in a row.

Or one hundred times. Nobody knows, because babies can't count.

At 1:30, Mama tried to cuddle with Baby again.

But Awake Baby doesn't need cuddles.

HA!

At 2 o'clock, Baby laughed at a joke only she understood.

At 2:15, Baby yelled a bit.

AHHHHHHHHH

HA HA HA HA

At 2:30, she laughed at her own yelling.

2:45—more yelling.

AHHHHHHHHHHHH

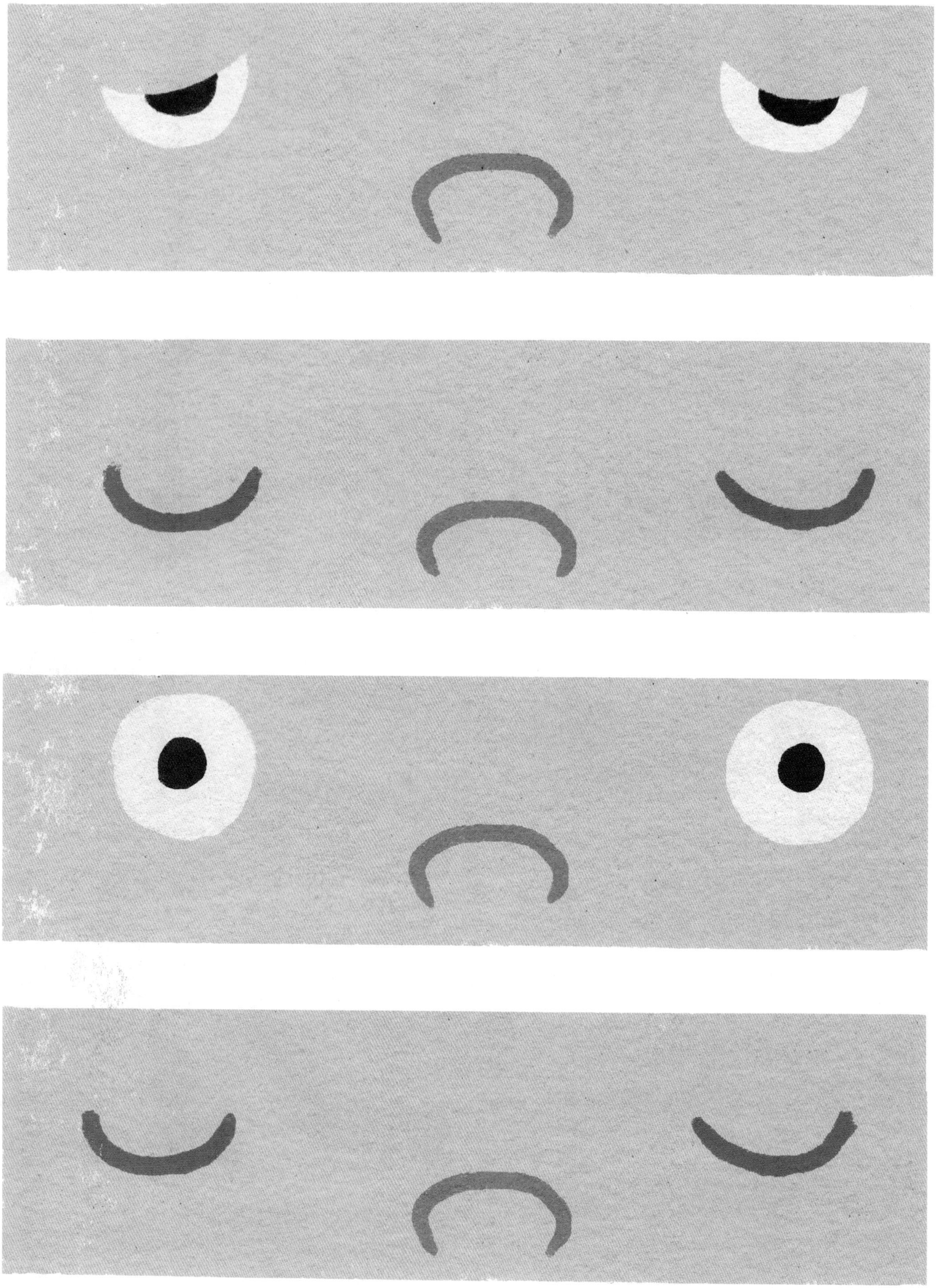

At 3 o'clock . . .

Baby's eyes . . .

began . . .

OMG!

to blink.

And in the darkness,
she saw a whole universe
of glittering stars.

Exploring the wonders of the universe
was the perfect thing for this baby to do,
because in space, no one can hear you scream.

Or sing.

Or throw a dance party.

At 4 o'clock, Mama carefully lowered Baby into the crib.

Baby let out a small sigh . . .

but stayed fast asleep.

HA!
Yeah, right!
Not this baby!

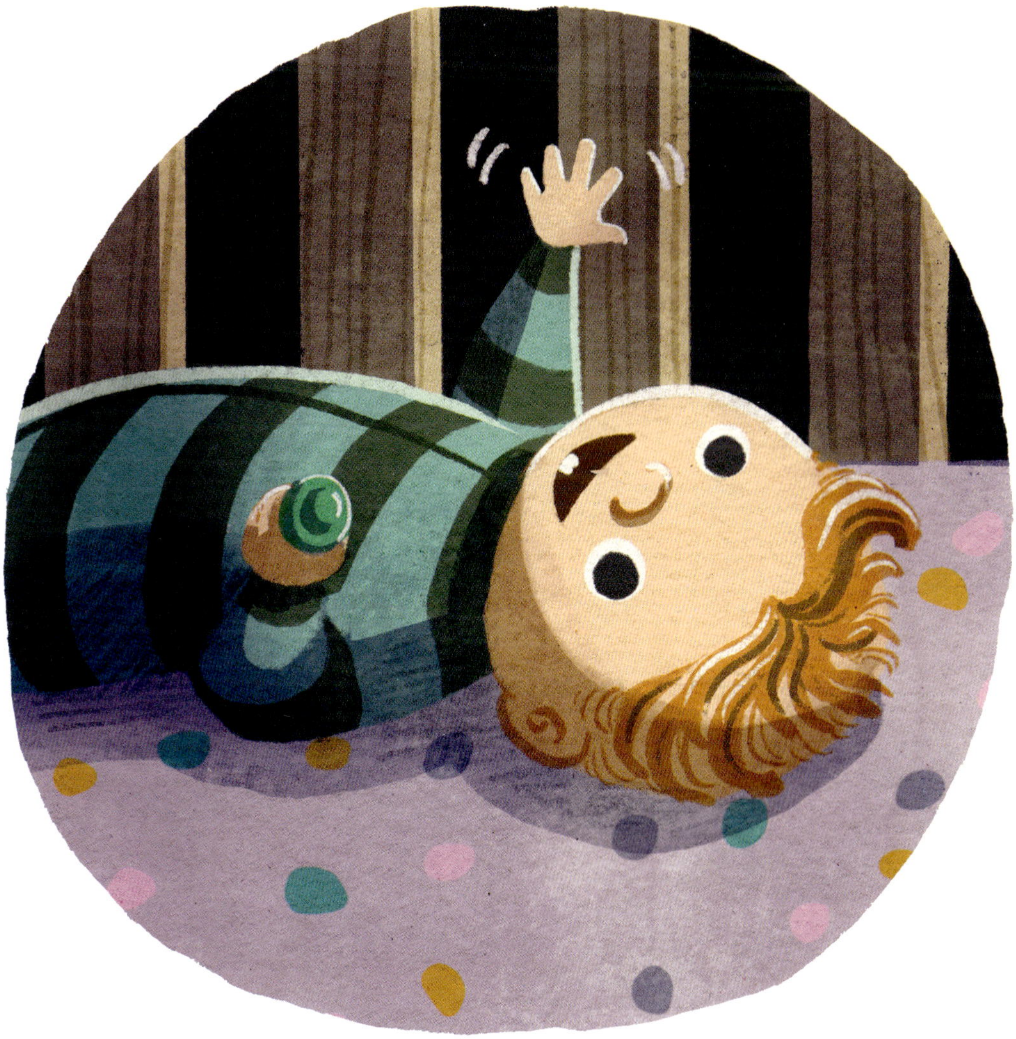

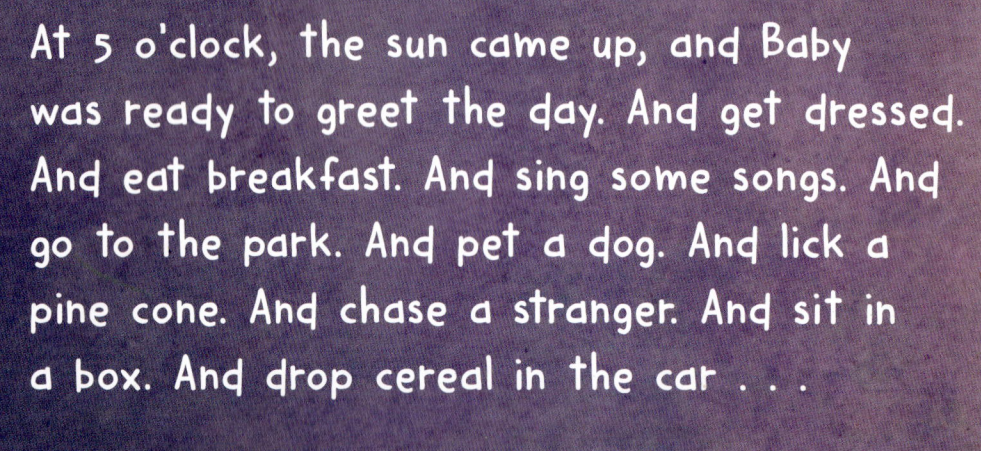

At 5 o'clock, the sun came up, and Baby was ready to greet the day. And get dressed. And eat breakfast. And sing some songs. And go to the park. And pet a dog. And lick a pine cone. And chase a stranger. And sit in a box. And drop cereal in the car . . .

. . . just as soon as her lazy family woke up.